BEACH LANE BOOKS

An imprint of Simon & Schuster Children's Publishing Division

1230 Avenue of the Americas, New York, New York 10020

Copyright © 2013 by Keith Baker

BEACH LANE BOOKS is a trademark of Simon & Schuster, Inc.

For information about special discounts for bulk purchases, please contact Simon & Schuster Special Sales at 1-866-506-1949 or business@simonandschuster.com.

The Simon & Schuster Speakers Bureau can bring authors to your live event. For more information or to book an event, contact the Simon & Schuster Speakers Bureau at 1-866-248-3049 or visit our website at www.simonspeakers.com.

Book design by Sonia Chaghatzbanian

The text for this book is set in Abadi.

The illustrations for this book are rendered digitally.

Manufactured in China

0713 SCP

First Edition

10 9 8 7 6 5 4 3 2 1

Baker, Keith, 1953–

My octopus arms / Keith Baker.—1st ed.

p. cm.

Summary: Little Crab asks what an octopus can do with his eight arms and gets a surprising, rhyming, reply.

ISBN 978-1-4424-5843-7 (hardcover)

ISBN 978-1-4424-5844-4 (eBook)

[1. Stories in rhyme. 2. Arm—Fiction. 3. Octopuses—Fiction.] I. Title.

PZ8.3.B175My 2013

[E]—dc23

2012040636

my Octopus arms

Keith Baker

Beach Lane Books
New York   London   Toronto   Sydney   New Delhi

Octopus, what can all your eight arms do?

Oh, Little Crab,
let me show you!

My arms can knit a sweater,

write a letter,

bake a pie,

and wave good-bye.

My arms can . . .

tie a bow,

perform a show,

strum a chord,

and saw a board.

My arms can do all this—and more!

My arms can . . .

drag a stick,

and take a photo—*click, click, click!*

My arms can . . .

stir the pots,

untangle knots,

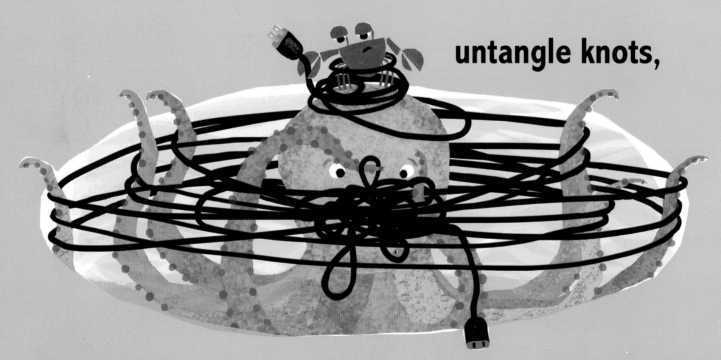

tip a hat,

and swing a bat.

Yes, my arms can do all that!

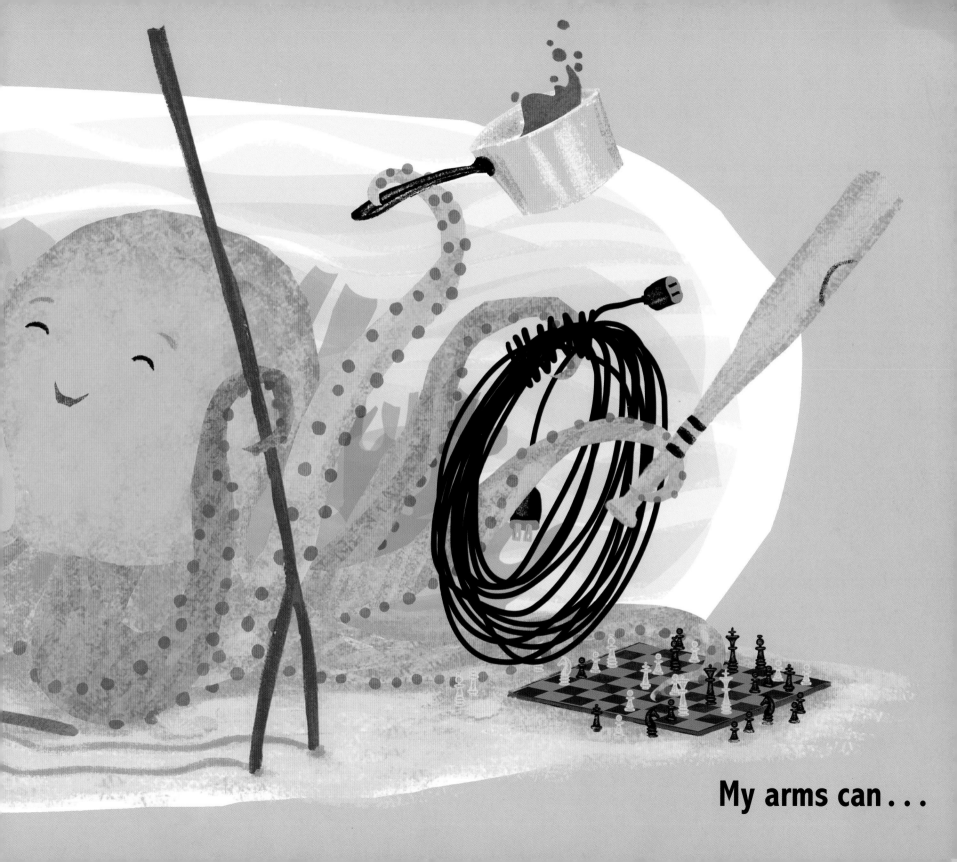

My arms can . . .

pull on socks,

unlock the locks,

dig a hole,

and climb a pole.

My arms can . . .

catch the fishes,

wash the dishes,

build a wall,

bounce a ball,

play a sport of any sort—
my arms can do it all!

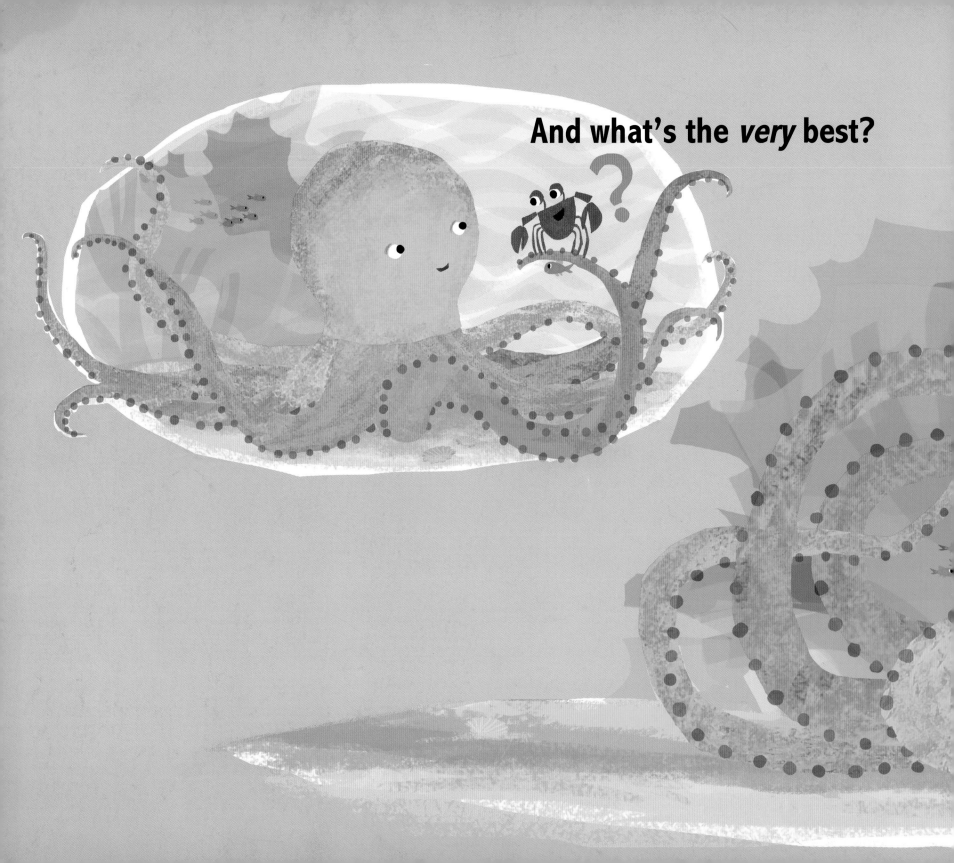

Well, did you know
that my octopus arms can grow...

and grow...

to reach out wide

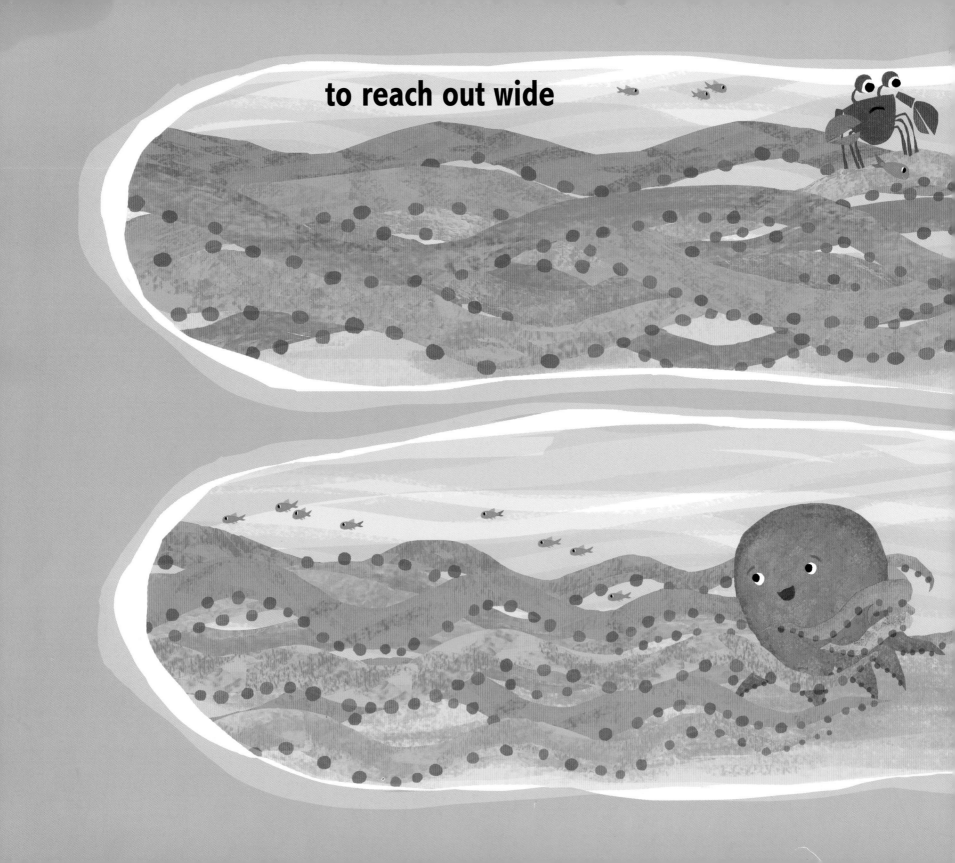

and pull somebody to my side.

With a hug—not too tight!—

my arms can make it
feel all right.

My arms can do this anytime.
All arms can—

yours *and* mine.

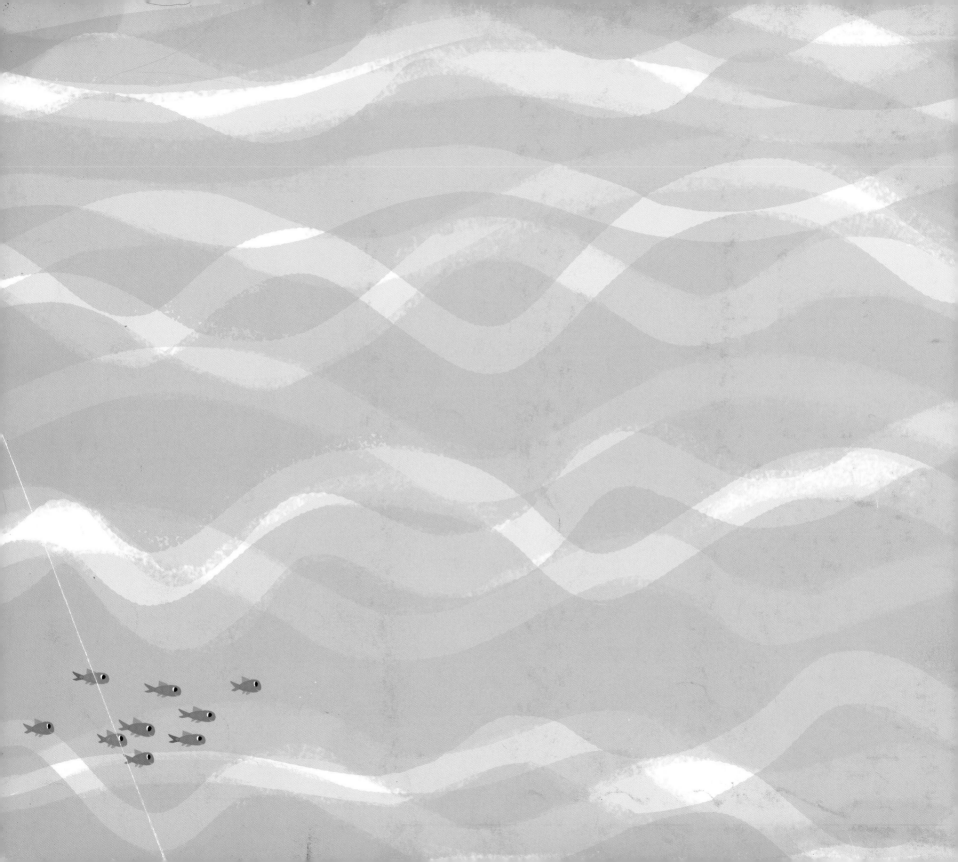